Sky Ship

and other stories

Geraldine McCaughrean

Illustrated by Ian McCaughrean

BLOOMSBURY EDUCATION

BLOOMSBURY EDUCATION
Bloomsbury Publishing Plc
50 Bedford Square, London, WC1B 3DP, UK

BLOOMSBURY, BLOOMSBURY EDUCATION and the Diana logo
are trademarks of Bloomsbury Publishing Plc

First published in Great Britain in 2004 by A& C Black, an imprint of
Bloomsbury Publishing Plc

This edition published in Great Britain in 2020 by Bloomsbury Publishing Plc

Packaged for Bloomsbury by Plum5 Limited

A catalogue record for this book is available from the British Library

ISBN: PB: 978-1-4729-6781-7;
ePDF: 978-1-4729-6780-0; ePub: 978-1-4729-6782-4

2 4 6 8 10 9 7 5 3 1

Printed and bound by CPI G

All papers used by Bloomsbury Publishing Plc are
forests. The manufacturing processes conform

To find out more about our authors and books

For Richard and David

Contents

Sky Ship

We look down into the sea and think of mermaids looking up at us – looking up at a surface mottled with sunlight. But, if you think about it we are like the mermaids. We too have a ceiling of blue overhanging our heads. True, it is higher than the tallest building – but then parts of the ocean are countless storeys deep. Just suppose that we too live in a kind of an ocean – an ocean of air – and that above us glitters and shifts the sunlit blue of yet another sea – a sea-in-the-sky. There was a time when our ancestors believed that the rain leaked out of that freshwater ocean, through imperfections in the baggy clouds; that our birds were the fishes of that upper ocean. What is more, they believed that ships sailed on that upper ocean, crewed by skymen and skymaids. Once or twice in the long history of incredible events, the two worlds even met.

* * *

One dankly overcast Sunday morning in the year of 1214, people came spilling out of church, yawning and stretching themselves after a two-hour sermon. They were just turning for home when a sudden clang and a sprinkling of stone dust made them look up. Something had struck the church tower, CLANG. BANG. It was still there, jarring against the stonework, chipping the waterspouts.

An anchor.

Its flukes scraped off birdlime and prised out mortar. Then, just as it seemed about to swing clear, it twirled once more in mid-air and snagged a window halfway up the tower.

The anchor cable, reaching up and away, far out of sight, twanged taut and a noise of groaning timbers came from beyond the clouds. There were shouts too, and no mistaking the anger and confusion in the voices, though the language was like none spoken on Earth.

The vicar was worried about the damage to his church, but the rest of the congregation stood spellbound, gazing upwards, as unseen hands tugged to free the snagged anchor of an unseen ship. At every tug, the anchor writhed in the window, but only wedged itself more tightly than ever.

Suddenly Jack, standing among the gravestones with his father, pointed upwards and shouted, "Look there! A foot!" And someone else cried, "A man!"

Through the low cloud and down the rope came a sailor, climbing hand-over-hand. His cheeks a-bulge, his eyes screwed almost shut, he clambered down the anchor cable, holding his breath. Jack's father, Caleb, shook his head in sympathy. He was a sailor and he, too, in his time, had been sent over the side of a ship to free a snagged anchor. As he told Jack, "When a captain needs dangerous work doing, a sailor's life is cheap."

Redder and redder the man's face grew, bluer and bluer the veins in his throat. His foot caught the wind vane. The brittle metal snagged the cloth of his trousers and, as he struggled to pull free, the anchor cable wrapped itself around him and he, like the anchor, was snagged.

"He's drowning!" yelled Jack. The crowd boggled at him. Foolish boy. How could a man drown in the fresh air?

"He's right!" exclaimed Caleb. "His kind don't breathe air!"

Then ten sets of feet were pounding up the tower stairs, setting the rungs rattling, setting the church booming with echoes. The anchor, jutting in at the window, blocked their path. They wrestled to free it, but it was wedged fast. By the time they squirmed past and reached the roof, the poor sailor lay gasping on the parapet, three-quarters dead from drowning.

Quick as a whip, Caleb and his son Jack snatched out their knives and began sawing at the rope. Aboard the sky ship someone shouted a muffled command. The words were strange but the meaning was plain as day to Caleb. "Captain's calling for an axe to cut free the anchor."

"What? With his own man still down here?" Jack was horrified. He sawed at the rope so hard that his fingers began to blister.

Caleb pulled a face. "He has to put the life of his ship above the life of one man. This one's only a sailor, after all, isn't he? Only a sailor like me." Strand by strand they hacked through the thick anchor cable. Above their heads the captain's cries became more angry and more urgent. Perhaps the crew of the sky ship was purposely slow in fetching the axe – thinking of the comrade they would cut loose, along with the anchor. Even so, what tide-rips or wild waves were battering the sky ship, pinioned as she was by her own anchor, unable to break free?

"I'm nearly through!" cried Jack, and Caleb threw his knife aside and lashed the drowning man to the anchor cable using his own belt. Before the knot was even tight, Jack cut the last strand of rope and the sky sailor was lugged skywards between them, like a puppet jerked offstage by its puppeteer. Unseen hands aboard the unseen ship were hauling in both cable and man.

"*I'm going up there!* I'm going to see the sea in the sky!" cried Jack. He jumped on to the parapet and caught hold of the rope. To have caught a glimpse of another world and to let it slip through his fingers was more than Jack could bear. But, as he swung into the air, his father grabbed him by the legs. "Let go, Father! I must see what's up there!"

"*Help me!*" cried Caleb, and the sexton and the carpenter and the vicar all stumbled across the roof and grabbed hold of Jack's legs as the sky ship's anchor chain swept him away. With four grown men dragging on his legs, it was impossible for Jack to hold on. With a sob of frustration and despair, he dropped back down on to the tower roof, clamping his hands under his armpits to ease the pain of the rope burns.

"*You should have let me go!*" he raged. "You should have let me see that sky ship! I would have been the first! No one has ever seen what's up there!"

Caleb sank his fingers in his son's damp hair. "And do you know what would have happened if you had gone? Do you? Do you? The very next cloudburst would have dropped you down dead at your mother's feet like a drowned kitten. *Think, boy!* You can't breathe sky water, any more than they can breathe our air. Let it go, son. Let it go."

And they stood watching – like mermaids on a reef – as the clouds above their heads buckled and bulged, and the unseen ship set an unknown course across the ocean-in-the-sky.

For many years, the anchor stayed wedged in the church tower window, a tantalising souvenir of an encounter with an alien race. The vicar (who discouraged such talk) told visitors that it dated back to a hurricane, a great tempest, when cows and carts and ships and anchors were blown into the treetops and left hanging from the spires. But his congregation knew better. Wonders such as that cannot be glossed over.

As for Jack, he took to watching the swallows swoop and glide in shoals through the higher reaches of the sky. And when, like his father, he became a sailor, he would often astound his fellow crew by climbing to the mainmast top, to be closer to the sky. He was always hoping, he said, to glimpse a keel,

a whale, a swimmer, a raft afloat in the sea
above him.

The incident of the sky ship was recorded by
Gervaise of Tilbury who, despite his name,
lived in Arles, France, in the thirteenth century,
and took a lifelong interest in witches and the
supernatural.

Breathless

Hannah and Hettie and their brother Edward watched from a bedroom window as the guests arrived: all the regular members of the Lunar Society.

"There's Frank," said Hannah, pointing. "I'll wager you anything he ends up in the roses." The dreamy young man with his nose in a book had already strayed off the garden path and was meandering across the lawn, absent-minded as ever. The children watched spellbound as he headed for the rose beds.

"Mama says he has his mind on higher things," said Hettie.

"He won't when he sits on a briar!" said Edward.

Sure enough, the young philosopher and poet ploughed painfully in among the tea roses and looked around him, baffled as to how he had got there.

The full moon rose above the trees, a silver disc of miraculous brightness even though the Sun had barely set. "The Man-in-the-Moon's lantern is very bright tonight," said Hettie.

"The Moon is a rocky piece of debris spinning round the Earth," said Edward heartlessly. "It doesn't shine at all. That's only the sunlight reflecting off it."

"I know that," said Hettie, though she had her doubts and much preferred her own ideas of the Moon: a friendly face, a pale peachy fruit, the largest pearl in the world.

Each month, when the Moon was full, the amateur scientists and philosophers of the Lunar Society met for a lecture or a debate or a demonstration by some visiting expert.

"Doesn't that make them lunatics," suggested Hannah, "if they only come out when the Moon is full?"

"Or werewolves?" said Edward. But they did not let the grown-ups hear them say it. The grown-ups took their Science very seriously. This was the Age of Science, the Age of Reason. The grown-ups never tired of saying that.

"Look! Here comes the speaker!" cried Hannah, as a stranger climbed down from a carriage outside. "He has a lot of equipment. Oh! Do you think he does magic?"

It was true that the man looked more like a conjuror than a lecturer. He had with him all kinds of jars and boxes and pipes. Best of all he had a white cockatoo in a gilded cage. "Oh! What does he do with the bird? I want to see! I want to see!"

So did the others. They were not usually so anxious to hear the Lunar Society speakers drone on about Humanism and Magnetism, Rousseauianism and all their other "isms". But conjurors with white cockatoos were different again! "Do you think that Papa would let us watch tonight?"

Their mother said it was far too late for the children to stay up, but their father was rather pleased that they were showing an interest in the sciences at last. He smiled indulgently, and said they might stay if they did not fidget or make a noise during the talk. "Tonight Mr Savery is going to address us on the subject of vacuums," he said grandly.

By candlelight the travelling scientist set up his equipment on Papa's big desk: pumps and tubes and canisters, all surmounted by a large, upside-down jar. The candle flame threw its reflected image up into the dome of glass.

"He looks like the Man-in-the-Moon," whispered Hettie as Mr Savery lifted up the bell jar just like a thorn-lantern.

Under the glass dome he posted the white cockatoo, then quickly twisted the jar home again into its rubber seal. Children and adults alike gazed at the beautiful white creature raising and lowering its crest, stretching a tentative claw, boggling out at the audience. Even the skull Papa kept on his desk seemed to gape its hollow eyes at the bird in the bell jar.

Thomas Coltman and Mary Barlow glanced at one another to comment on the beauty of the bird, then forgot to look back, mesmerised by each other's eyes. Edward saw them, nudged his sisters and they giggled about it. Thomas and Mary were in love. Just lately, they did not seem quite as interested in Science as they once had been.

"Now although there appears to be only one item in the bell jar," Mr Savery was saying, in a rasping, sing-song voice, "there are of course two. There is the bird, and there is air – a gas of two major components: that is to say, nitrogen and oxygen. The air that we breathe is approximately seventy-eight per cent nitrogen and twenty-one per cent oxygen, and it is this critical mixture which enables us to exist on this planet. A relatively narrow band encircles the Earth, and beyond it is the great void of Space, without air, without the means of supporting life."

Frank, the philosopher and poet, considered the vastness of Space, the edgeless infinity of the night sky, the smallness of Earth within the merry-go-round of the solar system... He thought he might write a poem when he got home.

"What will occur, we must ask ourselves, if we extract the air from this jar, and it is to this end that I have attached a pump to the bell jar containing the bird..."

Mr Wright was sketching – a few sparse lines capturing the pyramid of equipment, the candle, the rudiments of the bird. The cockatoo began to flutter and spread its wings, as if to grant him a closer view of its feathers.

"As the air is removed from the jar," said Savery above the noise of the pump, "the air pressure outside becomes greater. A less substantial vessel – a tin, say, or a paper carton – would implode under the pressure..."

The members of the Lunar Society wrote down "implode" in their pocketbooks, then returned their eyes to the bird. Within the jar, the cockatoo gaped its beak to squawk, but made no sound.

"Sound is also absent," Mr Savery went on. "Without air to carry the sound waves, sound cannot travel. The vacuum is a silent medium."

The bird struggled to take off into the darkness surrounding it, but found glass barring its way. Its chest distorted, as if it was imploding.

"It can't breathe!" cried Hannah. "It has no air to breathe!"

"Precisely," agreed Mr Savery, giving her an encouraging pat on the head.

Edward had moved forward, eyes peering, mouth slightly open. The Secretary's wife remembered a reason to leave the room.

"It is not the lack of *nitrogen* which makes the vital difference. The *oxygen* is far more crucial. Within its body now, the blood which generally carries oxygen to all the major organs is becoming depleted. It grows less scarlet – hence the slightly blue tinge you will observe..."

"Let it go now, please!" begged Hettie, reaching up to tug at the scientist's cuff, but he pressed on manfully, not allowing the little girl or sentimentality to deflect him from his lecture plan.

Frank-the-philosopher looked at the dying bird and thought how life was a little like that bell jar, a fragile capsule surrounded by dark, the gradual ebbing away of energy and vitality, the inevitable end never far away... It made him melancholy just thinking about it. Thomas and Mary, on the other hand, had not really noticed what was happening, lost in contemplation of their coming marriage.

"Can you see the blueness in the tongue, Hannah?" asked her father. "Close observation is very important in Science."

Hettie buried her face in her sister's dress and sobbed wildly. "It's dying! It's dying! He's killing it! Don't let him kill it!"

The cockatoo staggered, reeled against the bell jar; its beak scraped the glass making a sound the bird itself could not hear.

Edward watched with that same look he had worn the day he burned a butterfly using a magnifying glass. It was amazing to see a thing die, without a blow, without poison, without a drop of blood...

"At this stage," Savery went on remorselessly, "most of the air has been removed from the jar. A candle would no longer have sufficient oxygen to burn."

The cockatoo's tongue flickered like a guttering flame, between silently screaming jaws. Hettie could feel her own breast ache, unable to draw breath because she was crying so hard. "Silly girl! It's only a bird!" her father said.

The cockatoo fell to the floor of the jar.

"Ah, but where is the Science which can rekindle life once it's extinct?" asked a member of the Lunar Society who, as a churchman, was more interested in the philosophical aspect. Through the window, the Moon looked on, like a face aghast, but if it called out, no one heard it, sealed as it was within the silent vacuum of Space.

The travelling scientist began to dismantle his equipment. Some talked animatedly of supper, though some were slow to take their eyes from the white heap of feathers in the bottom of the bell jar. Mrs Barstow blew her nose. Slowly, everyone made their way out of the room, talking, debating, asking questions of the visiting speaker. Soon only Hettie remained.

A representation of the painting "An Experiment on a Bird in the Air Pump" (1768) by Joseph Wright (1734-1797), which demonstrates that life cannot exist inside a vacuum.

She climbed up on the desk, dislodging the skull, which fell to the floor with a thud. The candle flickered dangerously close to her petticoats as she twisted off the glass dome. Lifting out the limp white bird, she carried it to the window; its head lolled in the crook of her arm as she cradled it. Then she laid it on the window sill, in the moonlight.

A cool breeze stirred the garden, moving the trees, ruffling the white crest. It blew in at the great drill-hole nostrils of the cockatoo – an uneven mixture of seventy-eight per cent nitrogen, twenty-one per cent oxygen. Perhaps her fingers had squeezed from the heart one final beat. Perhaps the bird's blood retained a few molecules of oxyhaemoglobin. Anyway, the cockatoo stirred. Its blue tongue changed to a deeper purple. A wing fluttered. Suddenly it was gone from the sill – transformed as if by magic into a ragged flicker of white, a savage shriek in the garden; a shape like that of a miniature angel spiralling towards the face of the Moon.

This story was inspired by a famous painting, "An Experiment on a Bird in the Air Pump" (1768), painted by Joseph Wright of Derby. Joseph liked to paint the world around him – people caught up in the Industrial Revolution; people caught up in the eighteenth-century thirst for Science and Reason. Many of his friends were members of the Lunar Society and it must surely have been at one of their meetings that he witnessed the experiment he chose to paint.

Solomon's
Carpet

The carpet in the Atchuck Town Museum had lost all its colour but for a residual pink – as though the hair had worn off the hide of some prehistoric beast and left the skin showing through. Here and there, the pile was gone altogether: the pattern barely showed at all. Most of the fringing – once attached by knots so intricate as to defy the cleverest fingers – had long since come undone and disappeared.

There were stains, of course: the red of wine, the brown of blood, the indelible stain of invisible inks: the spill and slops of centuries. For the carpet had passed through many hands and many lands. Looters, merchants, thieves, exiles and collectors had all accounted it theirs. But it had outlived them, as it had outlived everyone who knew it for what it was.

Not that it was a thinking, sensate thing, of course. But it was responsive to beauty – to the colours of a sunset, the sound of clapping, the quickening of heartbeats, the kick of fear. Above all, *words* stirred it, setting the pile rippling, much as fear lifts the hair on human skin. Once upon a time, its pelt had deadened the echoes of a palace while wisdom settled among its fibres, making the lambent flame of magic flicker.

For this was Solomon's carpet: the one that had covered the dais in the throne room of King Solomon's palace. Four bare circles marked where the feet of his throne had once rested. The pattern of tessellated footprints showed where his ministers had once stood, listening in awe to his words of God-given wisdom: ten thousand angels to his right, ten thousand djinn to his left.

Even now, words still had the power to move the carpet. If a song reached it where it lay rolled in a corner, its threadbare shoulders would rise and fall, rise and fall: a sleeper dreaming. Now, at last, Time and Accident had placed it in a corner of the Atchuck Town Museum where it leaned, like a sentry fallen asleep on duty.

* * *

The Atchuck Town Museum was owned and run by Mr Mirabar Tuli. He was such an enthusiastic collector that his trips to the markets and wharves and auction rooms left him no time to organise what he collected. He would do it (he told himself) when the public were hammering on the museum door, demanding to see his collection. Since this was yet to happen, Mr Tuli went on collecting, and the rooms of the Atchuck Town Museum went on filling up – with tea-trays and stuffed birds, runic stones and snuff boxes, mummified cats and camel saddles, books and tin plates, bones, clothes and cutlery and carpets.

Amid this maze of oddities Mr Tuli's son Spode struggled to find room to grow up. He had arrived free-of-charge in his father's life. So he was valued far less than the monkey teeth from Bali or the bellows from Kazakhstan which had cost good money. In fact, Spode feared his father might swap him one day for something more collectable – like a set of spark plugs or a fossilised shrimp. The only thing collectable about Spode was his name, which had been borrowed from the base of a china teapot. The teapot was listed in the museum catalogue: *tea set, Spode (5 piece) [slightly chipped]*.

Spode-the-boy could never be catalogued: *Tuli, Spode (11) [liar and trouble-maker]*

Mr Tuli hated liars. He hated them more than people who sneezed over him in the street; more than young women who combed out their dandruff aboard public buses. Liars ranked just above shoplifters and below drunkards. Having caught his son in the act of lying, Mr Tuli was collecting up grains of forgiveness in the hope of one day liking the boy again. In the meantime, Spode found it best to hide out between the ottomans and armour, and secretly to read.

The fragility of the fans, mâché masks and blown eggshells had made Spode's early childhood a nightmare of shouting:

Be careful of that, boy!
Mind where you are treading, boy!

Don't run!

Now look what you've done, stupid boy!

But the stillness Spode had learned by the age of seven did not save him from his father's temper. For Spode liked stories: he liked to read them and he liked to make them up. He made up stories about the dragons on the Chinese vases; about the statues, about the swords on the wall and the rubber snake behind the door. In his father's book, that made Spode a liar. For Mr Tuli was devoted to facts. He bought items for the museum in the hope they would add to the world's sum of facts. *Story* books he only ever bought brand new, still shrink-wrapped, and never if pages were missing or dog-eared or someone had written their name inside.

Only Spode was stupid – and wicked – enough to read the words. Knowing full well his father's loathing of fiction – "Is it *true*, boy? Is it a *fact*, boy? It is not. It is *lies! All lies!*" – Spode could not resist the lure of the bookshelves. Whenever he thought his father was too busy to notice, he would curl up, between the stuffed emu and the Peruvian handloom, and secretly, wilfully break the rules laid down by his father. He would *read stories*.

One day he read a story about the Elephant's Child and how it got its trunk, and the story made him laugh out loud. Terrible mistake!

"What's the matter with you, boy? What's so funny?"

That was how Mirabar Tuli found out that his son had been opening – actually opening – the books on the museum bookshelves – cracking the spines back! – wearing out the print by running his eyes over it! Mr Tuli rent *The Elephant's Child* apart page by page, beat Spode, locked him up in the museum and went home without him, cursing disobedient boys.

Sweating with fear and indignation, Spode snatched down another book from the bookshelf – partly in defiance, partly to smother his sorrows and pain with a comforting story. Unfortunately, there was too little light even to read the title. Spode looked around for a lamp, but could find only a Russian Orthodox sensor. When lit, it shed little light but clouds of reeking smoke. Spode sat down in his usual place but, as day turned to night, cold-blooded, reptilian draughts crawled all over him.

So he unrolled the carpet that had stood propped against the wall for as long as he could remember. He spread it out flat, and its creases subsided round him like a stormy sea. Four round, bare circles marked where the feet of some great chair had worn clear through the weave. He sat inside the square they made – on the exact spot where the chair had once stood.

The book was hard. It was adult. Spode needed to hold the nouns in his mouth to defrost before they made sense. And so, lips moving, breath vibrating in his throat, Spode read out loud to the dead contents of the Atchuck Town Museum.

Words dropped from his lips on to the carpet and, like hair fastened too long in a band, the pile of the carpet turned painfully in its follicles. A thousand museumy smells plucked at the warp. The weft felt the small pulse beating in Spode's ankle. But above all, the acrid stench of injustice raised the carpet's hackles, roused its entire velvety nap, as cold raises goosebumps on human skin.

It rippled. The carpet rippled. Spode felt it, blamed the draught, and went on reading. Then his eyes drifted to the pattern on the carpet, those tessellated footprints: gold to one side, scarlet to the other; like the board for some complicated game. Idly he began to count the footprints, but it was harder than he had expected.

So now numbers too fell from Spode's lips on to the carpet, like warm rain. Worn patches sprouted new fibres. The stains – of blood and wine and asses' milk – grew damp again and rancid. Then, with a noise like a plague of locusts, the footprints were covered one by one, by the feet that had made them.

The men of gold seemed to wear huge golden shields across their backs, and helmets of coppery chain. But the "shields" pulsed with blood and, when unfurled, were fledged with brazen feathers flexing in time to a single, synchronised heartbeat. Wings! The helmets were shining coils of unkempt hair, tossing like the manes of impatient horses. The faces all shared the same ferocious beauty.

Spode might almost have succeeded in counting the footprints, but the ranks of gilded giants, who towered over him now, could no more be numbered than birds circling in a flock, or silver, shoaling fish. Their wings whispered the syllables of innumerable languages. How was it possible for such a host of figures – all larger than the statues in the town square – to fit inside the poky rooms of the museum? And how was it possible to survive their fierce loveliness?

Spode turned to crawl away from the trampling of their golden feet upon the golden footprints... and was confronted by a scarlet Alhambra of columns swathed in hissing silk. For the scarlet footprints that patterned the other half of the carpet were now all occupied by the feet of red-trousered djinn.

Turbanned with smoke and armed with curved swords and whips, they seethed like trees engulfed by forest fire. Tree-tall and varying in colour from mahogany brown and ebony black to ash-white albino, the djinn gleamed with sappy sweat and swayed with windswept frenzy, though their splayed feet stayed rooted to the carpet. How was it possible for such vast numbers to have crammed themselves into the dusty and cluttered museum? How was it possible to survive the terror smoking from their mouths or the magic rattling down from their clothes?

Spode coiled himself as small as he could, tying his legs in place with his arms, forcing his head between his knees. The angel hosts to his right, the spirit hordes to his left reached out to the edge of belief. The walls of the Atchuck Town Museum were no more solid than smoke, Mr Tuli's collection no more than the litter swept up by a cyclone. Beyond the walls, the town of Atchuck itself wavered into unreality. Overhead, a million blush-red birds were dismantling the roof.

The djinn did not so much as glance up. Instead, they turned their eyes on Spode – their glistening, fish-scale-silver eyes – and he saw his own face reflected over and over and over again, pale and terrified, hands held up to fend off their glares. Turning towards the angels, he saw himself reflected there, too: tens of hundreds of times, in their gilded, lidless, liquid unblinking eyes.

"Where is he? Where is Suleiman the Mighty?" the angels demanded to know. They asked it in languages long forgotten or never spoken, in the tongues of birds and of extinct beasts. They asked it in whispers and in song. *"Where is Suleiman the Mighty? Where is Solomon the Wise?"*

Behind him, the djinn had a question, too. He heard it with his eyes and ears and the inside of his brain. He felt it through the palms of his hands and the soles of his feet, finding its way in wherever sweat found its way out: *"Are you the Judge or the Judged? The Judge or the Judged? The Judge or the Judged?"* They unsheathed their swords. They bared their teeth at him through the tangle of their beards. The smell from the sensor was sickeningly strong. The carpet seemed to buckle under Spode's feet, then crack taut.

"*A wrong has been done here,*" said the army of angels.

"*We smell it,*" said the djinn, scraping the tips of their swords over the balding carpet. Warp and weft were laid bare like the wires of a complex musical instrument. And the ministers of Solomon began to peer about, as if for coins or needles mislaid deep in the pile. "*A wrong! A wrong! A crime for the punishing!*"

Spode looked, too, but all he could see, once his eyes strayed over the hem, was Atchuck town five hundred fathoms below, shrinking to the size of a stain on the warp and weft of the landscape. The carpet was flying.

"*Are you son of Suleiman?*" sang the angels in a great susurration of sound. "*Son of Solomon? A song made flesh? A Song of Solomon the Singer of Songs? Are you Suleiman's Son?*"

If he said no, would they throw him down to the ground? Would the carpet flex its back and buck him off, to his death? The birds overhead flew in such close convoy that they formed a canopy, blotting out the Sun, swathing him in their single shadow.

"*A wrong! A wrong! We smell a wrong!*" chanted the djinn, stamping at the carpet with first one foot and then the other, as if to break the ice on a frozen pond. When their myriad mirrored eyes fell on Spode's book, it burst apart in his lap: a dove in the talons of a hawk. The boards were peeled from the endpapers, the spine from its glue. Blowing papers billowed into the faces of the angels, who snatched them out of the air and ran their tongues over the print. The djinn crumpled the pages into balls, listening as they did so, holding the noise close to their long-lobed ears. "*A child! A father! A story! A crime!*"

"A JUDGEMENT! A JUDGEMENT! A JUDGEMENT FROM THE SEAT OF SOLOMON!" urged the angels, and ten thousand eyes turned on Spode Tuli. He would have shrunk from their gaze if he had not already been crouching as low as knees and spine and chin and chest allowed.

Spode was sure now that he was the criminal on trial. Hadn't he taken down a book, against his father's express command, and opened it and spoiled its newness and savoured its delicious lies? His crimes had caused this Court of Solomon to convene! And what defence could he possibly offer?

But as the seconds passed, the silence held, except for the rushing wind, and the wingbeats of the birds overhead. The angel host and the army of djinn went on staring at him, waiting for him to speak. Did they not realise, then, that he was the felon? Did their gold and silver eyes not see the guilt staining his conscience like an ember burn on a carpet? Might they even be mistaking him for King Solomon the Wise?

For one reckless moment, Spode considered pretending. Did he dare to stand up, speak in his deepest voice, pardon his own crime?

But when he had got to his feet – no easy matter on the rick-racking carpet – his mouth opened and words emerged unbidden:

"Judge for yourselves!" The voice was not even his.

With a noise like a weaver's shuttle, looks of consternation passed between the courtiers of Solomon. The angels drew back their heads; the djinn spun on their heels, swelling and diminishing in size as thought and unease passed through them. For a long time it seemed as if no one would speak aloud. Then words, like swarms of wasps, flew between angel and djinn, between the smoking mouths and manes of coppery hair, between the singing lips and long-lobed ears – words with fiery physical shape, words too fast to fasten on.

Just once Spode thought he heard: "... *disobeyed his father!*" and an answering shout of, "*...struck his son!*"

But then the argument began to crackle and spark too loud and bright for his ears and eyes to bear. Spode folded his face into his lap and covered his head with his arms, while the carpet swooped and plunged over eighteen colours of land and sea, and the blush-red birds screamed overhead.

It was the *click-click-click* of fibres parting that brought Spode to his feet again.

Under the intolerable trampling of angry feet, the antique carpet was starting to tear – gold ripping away from red. It did not happen slowly. The split came towards Spode like a spearhead, torn edges folding back behind it, to show glaciers and ice-fields below. It passed between Spode's feet and, with a bang, the hem-cord broke and the carpet split clean in half.

His legs went agonisingly in two directions, pulling him like a wishbone. The carpet began to spill him from between its two halves, like water from between cupped hands. He let out a cry.

Forty thousand eyes focussed briefly on him where he stood straddling a cubit of sky. Then angels and djinn turned back to face one another.

For a moment it seemed that the quarrel had turned to a brawl. For a black-palmed hand shot out and grasped a feathered wrist.

The angels reached out down-cuffed hands and grasped the djinn's black beards. But it was not fisticuffs. It was a darn – a clumsy stitching up of the tear. With forearms and whips, beards and hair and handfuls of clothing and turbans half unwound, the courtiers of Solomon held together the torn halves of his precious carpet.

Between Spode's ankles the ragged edges touched together, and King Solomon's carpet – though split in two – stayed in the air above a blue-green world...

Spode saw none of it. His eyes were tight shut. Not until the shabby raft had settled to Earth – the angels dissolved like spun sugar – the djinn swindled to smoke – the blush-red birds found camouflage amid the dawn clouds – did Spode dare open his eyes. Above his head, a tile chinked back into place.

It was as if the Atchuck Town Museum had been shaken by a distant earth tremor. Here and there a vase lay on its side. A stuffed owl had rolled over. A painting had slipped from its nail. And the balding pink carpet underneath Spode lay split in two from side to side.

Spode searched around in his head for a lie that might save him from his father's anger when Mr Tuli saw the carpet. No lie seemed big enough to cover the gaping slit, the ragged pink edges. Spode even considered telling the truth... but not for very long. A man who did not read stories could not be expected to picture this particular truth.

So he righted the fallen vases, rehung the picture of flamingos in flight, hid the wreckage of a book behind the bookshelf and propped up the stuffed owl on its single feathery leg. Rolling the red plush and gold, one into the other, he propped the damaged carpet back against the wall, where he had found it, hoping it might stand there, uncatalogued, for another dozen years.

Then he began thinking of those legions of ferocious angels, those djinn seething like so many volcanic geysers. What if he had folded them, cheek by jowl, sword by thigh, wing by whip...? Would they begin arguing again about the wickedness of boys and the unkindness of fathers? Would they begin to jostle and barge – throwing punches, throwing spells and curses and song and magic...?

Quickly, in a panic, Spode separated the two halves and re-rolled them at either end of the building. Given the general chaos of the place, there was a good chance his father wouldn't notice – at least for another decade.

By the time Mirabar Tuli arrived, it was as if nothing out-of-the-ordinary had happened at all in the Atchuck Town Museum.

Mr Tuli had not slept well. Fearful nightmares, he said, flinching from the memory. And a muscle strain, he said, rubbing his groin. Talk of a distant earth tremor, he said, on the National News: that must have been what did it – caused him to sleep so very... For once he did not lay the blame on Spode – not for the Earth's crust shifting or for the mysterious overnight strain to his wishbone. He did not dredge up Spode's crimes of the previous day. He simply cast his eyes uneasily about the museum's gloomy, cluttered rooms and went out early for his mid-morning coffee.

"While I am gone," he said, not quite meeting Spode's eye, "you can strip the shrink-wrap off those books up there. I heard it bends the covers."

That night, Spode was not obliged to sleep in the museum. So when, next day, he came to open up its doors, he knew he was not responsible for the lingering smell of smoke and sweat. He had swept up, so he knew there had been no feathers on the carpet the night before. He equally knew he had not married red to gold, footprints to footprints, angels to djinn. And yet the carpet stood now, as it always had, lolling against the wall like a sentry asleep on duty. And when he unrolled it – just far enough to see – he found no tear, no darn, no patching. Warp and weft must have... *interwoven* – as brambles do in a broken hedgerow, as nations do after a war, as rivers do after a drought, or families after a quarrel.

Wrapping his arms around the carpet – (it filled his whole embrace) – Spode heaved it back into place, then went back to stripping shrink-wrap from the books on the shelves. Since his father was late, he even risked glancing inside – just to see the lovely weft of words, the scarlet footprints left by a plot, the smoky shape of adventures... The day was muggy. He let the pages fan his face, pretending it was the wingbeat of passing wonders.

A fable appears in both the Koran and the Talmud concerning a flying carpet owned by the prophet Sulayman bin Daud (the Bible's King Solomon the Wise).

"It was of green sandal embroidered with gold and silver and studded with precious stones, and its length and breadth were such that all the Wise King's host could stand upon it, the men to the left and the djinns to the right of the throne; and when all were ordered, the Wind at royal command raised it and wafted it wither the Prophet would, while an army of birds flying overhead canopied the host from the Sun."

'Why Would
I Lie?'

Look at my hands. The rheumatism is so bad; they look as if I'm holding two fistfuls of stones. I dropped the quill just now and it took me ten minutes to pick it up again. I'd give the whole world for a new pair of hands. The whole world.

He was lucky. He went to his grave all but perfect. And so quick: like stepping through a door into another world. I cried like a baby the day my master died. To think I meant from the very start to murder him.

* * *

We set off from England on St Michael's Day 1322, on pilgrimage to the Holy Places – Sir John Mandeville and his manservant, Clym. Sir John was a learned man and a great writer-down of his thoughts. Nightly he wrote in his diary – except after a drop too much wine, when I wrote it up for him. He taught me to write, so I was able. That was useful: I knew I ought to be able to read and write if I was going to pass myself off as a gentleman.

During dinner Sir John would prop up a book before him and read out to me what other travellers had written about the next place on our route – Cyprus or Constantinople or Jerusalem. It was dull stuff, the way they wrote it. When we came to the places ourselves – pushing through the crowds, tripping over the beggars – Sir John would say, "They didn't mention the colour! They never said about the smell!"

We visited a *lot* of holy relics. Some days it seemed to me as if saints must explode at the point of death, and teeth and ribs and head and hands and blood scatter across Christendom for people to keep in silver caskets and venerate. A strange look came over Sir John whenever he visited holy relics. He seemed to be trying to see right through the gold and jewels to the thing inside – some anklebone or splinter of wood from Noah's Ark. "Astounding, isn't it," I said once, "that a piece of old hair can work miracles?"

"The question is, Clym..." said he, wearing that peculiar look of his, "... is it TRUE?"

I was taken aback. "Well, churches wouldn't *lie*, would they?"

"Hmmm," was all he said. He was a great stickler for the truth, Sir John. The times I heard him say, "Yes Clym, but is it TRUE?"

While he talked to monks and scholars about local history and politics, I preferred the company of sailors and travelling merchants. They told me the interesting stuff – what they had seen, what they had heard tell. Some of their tales made my hair stand on end, I can tell you! I met a sailor whose brother's cousin had seen furry men with heads like dogs. Another told me how, after three years at sea, he had sighted mermaids off the starboard bow. Mermaids! I told Sir John: "Shouldn't you put that in your book?" But he just looked at me with that same odd look. "Yes Clym, but is it TRUE?"

In the end, I collected my stories and he collected his. We would swap them at supper. He would tell me about some martyred saint whose head flew away, and I would tell him about the anthropophagi who don't have heads at all but keep their faces in their chests. He would tell me about some caliph murdered by his wife, and I would tell him about green river-monsters in Egypt that pretend to be logs then swallow down whole boats.

His smile was always so *doubtful*. Once I banged the table with my fist and shouted, *"What, then, do all your fine clerics tell the truth and all my sailors tell lies?"*

Next moment, I was scared. A servant, shouting at his master? But Sir John, bless him, he just smiled and said, "When we go there and see it, then I'll write it in my book."

"Can we go, then? *Can* we? You know how you read in some book that the world might be round? Well, we could go on and prove it. If we travelled right on round it, think what things you would have to write in your book! Folk would really want to read it, then!"

I can't think what made me say it. Already we had been travelling for two years, sleeping in pilgrims' hostels, camping under goatskins, sharing every plate of food with a swarm of flies. And here I was suggesting we go further, into unknown territories full of unknown dangers and the chance of getting killed. I must have gone mad.

Just for a moment, Sir John did seem to be tempted. Then he shook himself and poured another glass of wine. "I'm a man of property, Clym. I have lands, family, responsibilities. I haven't got years to spend on madcap journeys round the world."

My eyes filled with tears. I suppose Sir John thought I was sulky with disappointment, but actually I was remembering my plan.

I had meant, in some wild, out-of-the-way place, to cut his throat, put on his fine clothes, pocket all his letters of credit and go through the rest of life calling myself Sir John Mandeville. I had dreamed about it for months – how I would find some petty castle-court in France and marry some *duchesse* or *dauphinoise*, sending home to England once a year for more cash.

The world's a big place. Who would ever know?

But first I put it off because he was teaching me to read, then because he was teaching me

Latin and Greek. And then somehow I got fond of him. I'd put off murdering him too long, you see? That night in the Sinai desert, I realised I was never going to do it: I had grown to love the man. I could no more cut his throat than catch a unicorn.

The night before we set sail for England, I got talking to an old sea dog called Akbar. He wore his hair in a single grey plume rising from the top of his head and, as he was proud to tell me, he had made himself a fresh set of teeth entirely out of whalebone. I told him about our travels, and of course that set Akbar talking.

"I've seen a place where lambs grow on trees, like fruit," he said. "I was shipwrecked on the isle of Lodestone, which draws ships to it by the iron of their nails and wrecks them on its metal rocks! I've been to the country where each person has one great foot so large that he lies on his back in the shade of it."

Mesmerised, spellbound, I watched those whalebone teeth clacking. Just for a second I found myself thinking, "Yes, but is it TRUE?" Then I settled down to enjoy Akbar's stories, swallowing them down whole, like pilchards, between mugs of ale.

He had seen sea monsters, and lands where men and women go about stark naked; birds that talk and fish that glow in the dark. He had been in Borneo where jewels grow on the reed-stems. He fed me such a feast of facts, that when he started asking me questions, naturally I answered. I told him how Sir John was a prosperous gentleman, how we were setting sail next day, how we were sleeping in a store-room over the ironmonger's shop...

Sir John called me away then, or I would have talked more. My master said he had a present for me, so I instantly forgot Akbar and his tall tales.

It was a book. "A gift for my loyal secretary, apt pupil and excellent good friend," he said.

"Me, you mean?" I was woozy with wine, and too astonished to be gracious. I cannot begin to imagine what he paid for a copy of

John Plano Carpini. For *me*. For his excellent good friend!

"I am a poor adventurer, Clym," he said. "After two years, all I can think of is home and a yard of English ale. But you! You have the soul of a true explorer. Listen. If you want to go farther, go with my blessing. I free you from your employment. I'm sure I can weather one voyage on my own. Otherwise, come home to England with me, and sit in an armchair and read about the sights other valiant men put themselves to the pain of visiting. Eh, Clym? Which is it to be?"

My head was reeling. I could picture English orchards and Indian gems all at the same time; dog-headed men and Hertfordshire church steeples. "May I tell you tomorrow?" I said, clutching the book to my chest.

We bedded down in that comfortless store-room over the ironmonger's, surrounded by buckets, tools, nails, pots and pans and luggage, and went instantly to sleep.

I was woken by a single cry from Sir John.

The intruder was no more than a shadowy shape amid the darkness, but as he turned for the door, I saw the flash of whalebone teeth, unnaturally white. And Sir John's money-belt in his fist. I tried to tackle him, but he lashed out, and I fell against the wall.

Sir John was dead before I reached him – a single stab wound through the heart. For the rest of the night I sat there beside him in the dark, crying. I remember wondering what part I ought to keep as a relic of this good, gentle, witty, clever man.

In the end, I kept his letters of credit, naturally.

That fool Akbar, being illiterate, had left the most valuable prize – the books. In the morning, I put on Sir John's clothes, packed up the diaries, his copy of Herodotus, Pliny and Friar Odoric, and as much luggage as I could carry. I went aboard the first ship to sail – bound not for England but for France. I called myself "Sir John Mandeville, traveller and writer." It was easy. I became my master. It was as simple as that. Who in the world knew or cared enough to say any different?

* * *

That was thirty-four years ago. I am thinking to go home now – to St Albans, my home town. England is the best place to publish, the best place to grow old.

If my hands will let me, I'll just write the last line of this book of mine *"I, John Mandeville, saw this, and it is the truth."*

There now. The book is finished, and I venture to say there is no book like it in the world. Why did it take me so long to write? Well, an author must collect his material, mustn't he?

I've travelled halfway round the world – to Java and Sumatra, Ethiopia and India, Tibet and China and Tartary. I've lived in the palaces of emperors and dined on strange fish. And all the wonders I've seen are recorded here, in my life's work: The Travels of Sir John Mandeville. What? Why do you look at me like that?

Here you will read of men who are half-woman, of wilderness-people who grow horns and never speak, of giant snails and dog-headed men with tails, of lambs which grow on trees, and sons who cut off their father's heads at death to cook and eat; cyclopses with one eye set in their foreheads; Amazon warrior-women, and sultans who marry a dozen wives. Do you know, there is a forest of pepper trees in India twenty-three days long, and the kings there build castles on the backs of elephants?

Readers will gasp in amazement as they read, and wonder that the world can be so full of strangeness. Some will even ask, "Yes, but is it TRUE?"

To them I say, "Go and see for yourself! Why would I lie?"

* * *

Look at my hands – like two fistfuls of stones. I dropped the quill just now and it took me ten minutes to pick it up. I should employ a secretary, like that boy Clym so long ago in the Holy Lands. He looked a lot like me, they say: same ruddy complexion, same yellow ringlets. But he died young. Suddenly. I was there, and

I can vouch for the boy dying an easy death. It was just as if he stepped through a door into another world, to see what new wonders it had to offer.

The Voyages and Travels of Sir John Mandeville, Knight was published in 1371 as a guide book for pilgrims, based supposedly on the author's travels through the Holy Land, Africa and the Orient. Half seems to be genuine, the rest stitched together from sailors' stories, classical writings and other people's travel books. Some of the wonders described have a rational explanation – crocodiles, orang-utans, howdahs... others are simply silly.

Even so, world maps were redrawn on the strength of this book. Leonardo da Vinci owned a copy. Christopher Columbus was inspired by it to try sailing round the world. The King and Queen of Spain agreed to help him after they, too, read Mandeville. So, though much of the book is plainly fiction, the fact that it changed the world is no word of a lie.

The Lost
Birthday

Thomas was a clever boy, though not quite clever enough to understand why this made him unpopular. At school he was considered teacher's pet, because he learned everything the teacher taught and still thirsted for more. The teacher, Miss Trotter, might have liked him for this, if he had not kept asking questions she could not answer.

Old farmers who for decades had read the weather in seaweed and the colour of leaves did not seem to *want* to know what Thomas could tell them of cumulonimbus and barometric pressure.

When he stirred his mother's soup the wrong way – widdershins – saying, "Only people can be superstitious, not the soup," his mother slapped him.

Only his sister, Elizabeth, knew that Thomas was nothing but an ignorant boy. She was about to get married and naturally that meant she was too clever to bother with anyone, let alone Thomas.

So Thomas used to hang about near the inn and the seminary, and hold the reins of horses for lawyers while they drank, and run errands for doctors. He did it in exchange for information about the Magna Carta or the bones of the human body. And whatever he learned, he shared only with Gammer, his antique grandmother, who slept in a bed beside the fireplace. While he held her bowl, he fed her porridge and a diet of comets, biology, French and poetry. Since Gammer was seventy-nine and imminently expecting to die, she took in only the porridge.

It was Thomas who first heard tell of the alteration to the calendar. A traveller aboard the daily stage left his newspaper on a bench by *The Red Lion*, and Thomas took it home and read from it to Gammer – court engagements for the autumn of 1752, the war in Tibet, the invention of a lightning conductor...

"It says an act is going through Parliament to change the calendar, Gammer. To match the European one. By reason of the Earth taking 365¼ days to go around the Sun once, not 365."

"What's that? What are you babbling about, boy?"

"All those quarter-days have added up over the years. Seemingly, the Pope made things right in Europe centuries back, but we kept to the old style. Now we are grown eleven days apart from Europe. And Lord Chesterfield wants to jump us forward eleven days."

"Don't talk folly, child," mumbled Gammer. "A man cannot jump eleven days, no more than I can jump a five-bar gate. You have it all faddled in your brain."

But sure enough, at church the following Sunday, Reverend Persimmon broke the same news to the village. "An adjustment to the Julian calendar," he intoned, "bringing it in line with the Gregorian one." Impatient to get on to his carefully-crafted sermon, he did not trouble to expand.

As a result, no one listened to his sermon. A gradual crescendo of buzzing whispers swelled like a rising tide and washed away his oratory, until the Reverend Persimmon slammed shut his Bible and called for the last hymn.

"Cannot be true," said the whispers.

"Take eleven days off us? He's mistaken, truly."

"What man can do it?"

"Not the King himself."

"Only God, sure. Never Parliament."

"Not *eleven* days!"

"No, no. You don't comprehend," whispered Thomas. "It is a way of reckoning things, simply. You see, the world takes 365¼ days..."

But they were not listening.

The farmers were aghast. "How am I to finish harvest 'fore Harvest Festival, if you take me out eleven days?"

"'Tain't true, or me marrows would be coming ready for picking."

Mrs Baker clutched her mountainous stomach. "What, the babe due any minute and the crib only half made?"

Thomas's mother howled and held her head. "I feel it! I feel it! Eleven days nearer my grave!"

"Mam, you're no older than yesterday," Thomas tried to explain. "One day only. It's naught but a kind of arithmetic."

"Oh, hold your tongue, noddle!" she snapped, clipping his ear. "They rob us of our taxes and now they've robbed us of our days!"

Instead of walking directly home from church, the village gathered in the yard of *The Red Lion* to exchange outrage.

"Oh, but Mother!" cried Elizabeth, sailing against the tide of feeling. "It's wonderful! Do you not see? My darling will be home any moment. And in three days, I shall be a married woman. I am going to watch for his ship!"

"He just set sail, Lizzie!" said Thomas. "How can he get to Ireland and back in a day?"

But his sister only cast him a look of contempt and went to sit on a cliff top and await a ship not due back for a week.

Thomas ran to the rector's house. "Come quick, Reverend Persimmon, and explain to them about the calendar! My ma and all are acting like the Three Sillies, and I can't make them understand. They think they've lost eleven days out of their lives!"

Mr Persimmon, a beaker of claret in one hand, sniffed loudly. "Good. If they think they are brought nearer to Judgement Day, they may cast aside their sin the sooner," he said, and shut the door in Thomas's face.

By the time Thomas got back, the whole village was in uproar. Even Miss Trotter was quacking like a duck. "And if this be no longer Sunday, but Friday rather, why are the children not in school?"

Someone daubed a rude word on the rector's garden wall, and Dafyd Owen (who was a Baptist) called Persimmon "a lackey of those despots at Westminster".

"It is not Mr Persimmon's fault," Thomas told his grandmother. "They should not go blaming the rector for passing on the news."

"News? What news?" asked the frail little creature, her strength too small to allow her a turn of the head. Thomas began to explain yet again, but the door of the cottage was flung open and his mother burst in.

"*We are to lose eleven days from our lives, Gammer!*" she wailed, hair all awry and her face tear-stained. "And there's the wedding on top of us, and no time to do it, and the Sabbath's turned weekday, and those villains in London have delivered us whole days and days closer to the end of the world!"

"Gammer, take no notice. Ma doesn't..." said Thomas, but his mother came at him, swinging her bonnet by the ribbon.

"Eleven days gone are eleven days gone! Don't they bring rent day eleven days closer? And when you lie on your deathbed, my boy, you'll think it more than ill that those mongrels in London cut you off from the sweetness of light and breath eleven days too soon!"

"Eleven days?" Gammer sat up, her milky eyes brighter than they had been for a long time.

"What of my feast day? Am I not to be eighty?"

If her daughter had not worked herself into such a state of panic, she might have thought to say something soothing. But she was shrill with fright. "Just so! Just so! No birthday for you, Ma! You must be seventy-nine still, and Lizzie must be wed without cake or bakemeats, and there shall be no fair-going for Thomas!"

"No fair?"

"Well, and how should there be a mop fair without the day where the mop fair should have been? Eh, noddle? Eh?"

All of a sudden, Thomas felt less cheerful about the change to the calendars.

The yard outside was filled with wailing, as though the Last Day might indeed have come sooner than expected, and Elizabeth came in weeping and moaning.

"Ship's lost! He's gone, I know it! Or he's left me and found another in Ireland! 'Tis the fourteenth, they're saying, and we was to be married day after tomorrow and where is he? Still gone? *Gone! Drowned, or deserted me!*

He'll never come back, I know it, and I shall live an old maid all my days!"

His mother and sister fell on each other's necks in an apoplexy of grief.

"Be quiet, you gooses."

It was Gammer – and yet it was not Gammer. She had thrown off her blanket and was sitting on the edge of the bed, legs like dogwood, knees like crab-apples. "Do I stand there yammering on, and leave the corbies to do as they please? Not while there's breath in me!"

"Gammer!"

She was pulling a scarf over her thinness of hair – fingers like spillikins, knuckles like five-stones – and a cloak over her shift. "I set my mind to living eighty year on this Earth, and will some Westminster rake have me wait on eleven months more before I see a feast day? Nothing good ever came out of London, but this day's work we will push back down their throats! I'll take a broom to the King himself for stealing of my birthday!"

No spectre rising from its grave was ever so alarming as Gammer Coates the day she rose from her bed. Before anyone could restrain her, she was out in the lane, her piping voice exhorting the baker, the farrier, the sexton to "Rise up and rout the government, you lummocks!"

What with his sister weeping and wailing, and his mother on her knees praying for hell to swallow up the rector, Thomas felt obliged to go after his grandmother, if only to be at hand when she fell down dead.

But he found her well down the road, walking at the head of a band of malcontents, fuelled by indignation and deaf to all reason.

"Where are you going, Gammer?" he panted.

"To murder the King!" said the farrier, who had been solacing himself with home-made gin.

"All by yourselves?"

"There will be more like us!" declared Gammer. "No one will swallow such wickedness!"

"Come home, Gammer. Please!"

"Not till they give us back our eleven days!"

And before he knew what was happening, Thomas found himself swept along by their tidal wave of outrage.

In every town they came to, people who had been told the news (but not what to make of it) were reeling from the shock – people gnarled by old age or sickness, people who had already worked out the arithmetic of their lives and seen too many days gone from their allotted span to spare eleven more.

Thomas saw a side to his grandmother he had never seen before. All his life she had been the invalid beside the fire, silently, patiently awaiting her end. Now she was a firebrand, engaging total strangers in conversation, persuading them to revolution. The farrier and the baker turned back – they had trades to tend – but Gammer Coates trotted on, cheeks incandescent with zeal. And Thomas felt obliged to trot after her.

In Arrowby a doctor raised the shutters of his coach and asked about the commotion in the road:

"Give us back our eleven days!

Give us back our eleven days!"

He leaned through the window and shook his fist, calling Gammer "a mad old witch" and "a stupid, ignorant peasant".

Thomas was so incensed that he began running alongside the coach, banging on the paintwork, bawling at the top of his voice, *"She is not mad! She lost her birthday, didn't she? Can you give it her again? Can you put off rent day, either?"*

The doctor flushed purple, pulled down the blind again and shouted to the driver to put on speed. Thomas stumbled and fell behind. When he turned back, he was just in time to see Gammer Coates pick up a stone and throw it through the open window of the town hall. It landed in the mayor's soup.

* * *

Sitting in Arrowby lock-up, Thomas and Gammer Coates lost track of the hours. While they were there, Thomas had plenty of time to explain about the correction of the Julian calendar to bring it into line with the European Gregorian one.

But he did not try.

"The thing is," he said, "to take every heartbeat for a second. It's the only true, reliable clock." Then, on the wall of the lock-up he multiplied sixty by sixty and again by twenty-four to show Gammer how many seconds she had lived each day of her life; how many years, how many heartbeats. "And your heart has not ceased beating for eleven days, has it?" he argued. "Therefore you must have lived to your eightieth by now."

Gammer nodded reflectively, her smile huge as the calculations on the dank wall.

"But if we give 'em their way, they will have Christmas wrong ever after, boy – and New Year and fair days and the century's end..."

"It won't fret them," said Thomas confidently. "People are not fretted by what they don't know, only what they think."

And Gammer nodded again and patted his hand.

When the circuit magistrate arrived, Thomas and Gammer were brought out of the lock-up blinking, to stand trial for riotous behaviour. When asked her age, Gammer did not hesitate.

"Eighty years today, Your Honour. We counted the heartbeats, we did."

"Eighty!? Why, what is the constable thinking of, arresting a gentle woman of eighty?" demanded the magistrate, frowning about the courtroom through his eyeglasses.

The constable rose to his feet, flustered. "I never thought she was above sixty, sir, honest!"

At which Gammer Coates beamed, radiant with happiness.

"I sentence you both to eleven days," said the magistrate deliberately.

Thomas gulped. The lock-up was a very damp and unwholesome place for an old lady to pass one night, leave alone a week and a half.

"But in consideration of your feast day and your great age," the magistrate continued,

"I stipulate that those days run twixt third September and fourteenth September in this year of our Lord 1752... All supposing those days can be found."

He did not exactly wink, but the clerk of the court coughed, and the beadle snickered, and Gammer Coates beamed all the wider.

"You're a good man, sir!" she told the magistrate. "My granddaughter's marrying in a heartbeat or two. If you're passing by Grovely way, we'd be right honoured if you'd set down your bum 'twixt me and the groom."

"You are kind, madam," said the magistrate with a gracious nod. "You are more than kind."

"That's if the lad is fool enough to come back from Ireland," Gammer whispered to her grandson.

For ease of counting, we tend to say that there are 365 days in the year, but in fact it takes the Earth 365 1/4 days to circle the Sun. (We make allowances for it now, with Leap Years, but they are a relatively modern invention.) Rome adjusted its calendars, but England was slow to follow, so the English calendar gradually slipped out of step with the European one. By 1752, it was eleven days adrift. Lord Chesterfield tore eleven leaves off the calendar – 3-14 September – to put things right.

But ill-informed, uneducated people could not grasp his explanation. Up and down the country, riots broke out as people found themselves eleven days further through the year without understanding why.

So this story could have taken place in any number of villages, in any number of English shires, in the year 1752.

Glossary

Alhambra: a heavily ornamented palace in Granada, Spain, dating from the thirteenth century.

anthropophagi: cannibals.

caliphs: the rulers of the Islamic world.

Christendom: this is an old word for Christianity; it is also the collective term for Christian people throughout the world.

dauphinoise: the wife of the direct heir to the French throne.

djinn: a mythological spirit with supernatural powers who can take on human form.

humanism: a philosophical movement which values the importance of human reason over the authority of the Church.

Magna Carta: Dating from 1215, this documented the priviliges and rights of both the church and freemen in England.

pilgrimage: a journey to a sacred place, usually for religious reasons.

orthodox: conforming with existing behaviours and beliefs.

Rousseauianism: the movement founded by the French philosopher Jean-Jacques Rousseau (1712-78) who believed that man was naturally good but whose goodness had been spoilt by society. His ideas strongly influenced the republican, anti-church French Revolution (1789-99).

scimitar: a sword with a curved blade that widens towards its point.

sexton: a church caretaker, who often doubles as a grave-digger and bell-ringer.

sultan: the ruler of a Muslim country.

READING ZONE!

TOP READING TIP

When reading books with several different stories in them, it can be a good idea to have a break after you've read each one.

It can feel strange to carry straight on as each story has a unique setting and characters.

When you come to the end of a story, think about it and about what the author is trying to tell you.

You could even find someone to talk about it with before you carry on and read another one.

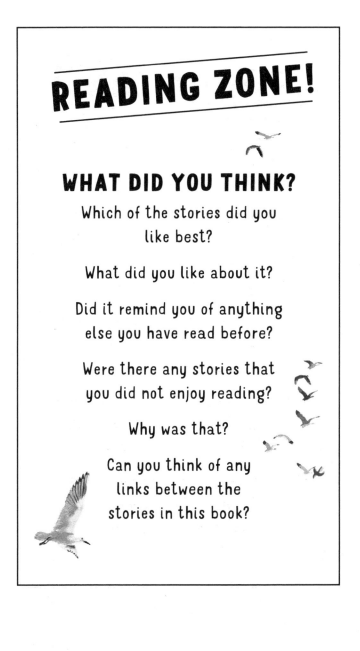

READING ZONE!

WHAT DID YOU THINK?

Which of the stories did you like best?

What did you like about it?

Did it remind you of anything else you have read before?

Were there any stories that you did not enjoy reading?

Why was that?

Can you think of any links between the stories in this book?

READING ZONE!

GET CREATIVE

Think back to the first story in the book. What would it be like if there was a world in the sky above ours?

Why not try writing a story as if you were Jack and *did* manage to go up the rope to the new world. What might you have seen?

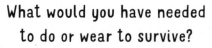

What would you have needed to do or wear to survive?

Who might you meet?

Be as imaginative as you can, and remember that the first story in this book might help you with some details of what the world would be like.